THE KIDS OF EINSTEIN ELEMENTARY
TITANIC CAT

Written by
Len Mlodinow & Matt Costello

Illustrated by **Josh Nash**

Cartwheel
B·O·O·K·S ®

SCHOLASTIC INC.

New York   Toronto   London   Auckland   Sydney
Mexico City   New Delhi   Hong Kong   Buenos Aires

For Alexi
—L.M.

Dedicated to the First Graders of the
William O. Schaefer Elementary School...
past, present, and to come!
—M.C.

Text copyright © 2004 by by Matt Costello and Len Mlodinow.
Illustrations copyright © 2004 by Josh Nash.

All rights reserved. Published by Scholastic Inc.
SCHOLASTIC, CARTWHEEL BOOKS, and associated logos
are trademarks and/or registered trademarks of Scholastic Inc.

Library of Congress Cataloging-in-Publication Data is available

0-439-53774-6

10 9 8 7 6 5 4 3 2   04 05 06 07 08

Printed in the U.S.A. • First printing, July 2004

Contents

Chapter ONE

Kenny, José, and Steffi walked downstairs to the school basement. Slowly, quietly, they walked past old computers, wires, batteries, and books.

"There they are," Kenny whispered. He pointed at what looked like a row of outdoor toilets. But these "toilets" were really time machines that could take them to *anytime, anywhere!*

The kids had already been back to the time of the dinosaurs, where they had met a baby dinosaur named Sammy.

Now they wanted to go back in time to see Sammy again.

"Uh-oh," José said. He picked up a note taped to one of the machines. José read it aloud.

To the kids of Einstein Elementary…
I'm warning you: Keep away from my machines!

Signed, ME

"Um, maybe…" said Kenny. "Maybe we'd better not go."

"I don't care what 'me' says," Steffi said. "I want to visit Sammy!"

"I'm with you," said José.

José stepped into one of the Einstein machines. Steffi followed.

Kenny looked around the dark basement. He didn't want to stay there alone! He rolled his eyes and walked

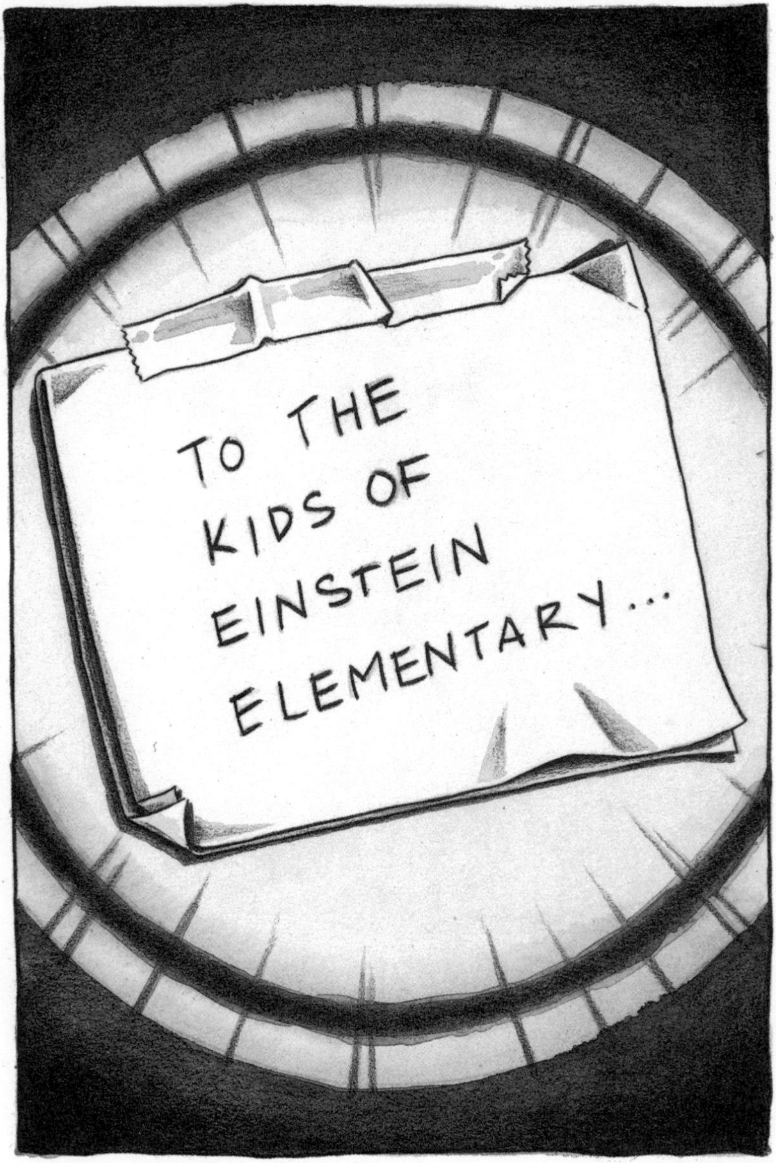
TO THE
KIDS OF
EINSTEIN
ELEMENTARY...

into the machine.

José looked down at the controls. One lever had the labels HERE and THERE. The other lever had the labels NOW and THEN. And a big switch had a label that read: DO NOT *EVER*, **EVER** THROW THIS SWITCH.

Steffi looked at the controls, too. To her, something looked wrong, very wrong.

"Wait!" she yelled.

But she spoke too late. José had already thrown the switch.

Outside, the box bounced up and down. Inside, nothing seemed to move at all. But the kids felt as if they were spinning on a carnival ride.

"Woooowwww!" yelled José.

Tiny tornadoes of purple smoke formed near their feet. Kenny tried to keep away from them.

Then the box stopped moving—both

inside and out. Everything was very, very quiet.

"Steffi? Steffi…why did you say, 'wait'?" Kenny finally asked.

"The controls weren't set the way they were last time. We didn't go to the time of the dinosaurs!" she said.

The kids looked at each other, now scared. They could be anywhere in space or time.

"Well, we can't just stay here," said José. He slowly opened the door and stepped outside.

Chapter TWO

José looked around. Steffi was right. This was *not* the land of the dinosaurs. This was somebody's bedroom!

Kenny stepped out, too. He looked around the elegant, old-fashioned room. "Where are we?" Kenny said. "And when?"

Steffi was the last to leave the machine.

"The controls were set to a different THERE, and a different THEN. From the look of the furniture, I guess we are back about one hundred years," she said.

"Well, I'd say it's around...April 14,

1912," said José.

"Nice try, José. But I don't think you can guess the *exact* date by looking at the furniture," said Steffi.

"No," he said, "but I can by reading this!"

José picked up a letter off a dresser and started to read.

April 14, 1912

Dear Dad,
Mom and I are finally on our way. I miss you so much already. I'm glad I have the box with the puzzle lock that you invented. Will the puzzle lock make us rich? I hope so. I can't wait to meet you in America.

Mittens misses you, too.

Love, Emma

Kenny held up a photo he found on the nightstand. "This must be Emma and her dad," said Kenny. "And Mittens."

The photo showed a young girl sitting on a man's lap, and holding a cute gray cat.

Steffi picked up a pretty wooden box from the dresser.

"I wonder what's in this?" said Steffi.

The box had a lock with four dials. To unlock the box, you had to turn four dials to just the right number. Each dial went from one to ten.

Steffi started dialing different numbers.

"You'll never open it that way," said Kenny. "There are ten times ten times ten times ten different possibilities."

"That's ten thousand!" said Steffi.

You can think of the secret combination for the four dials on the lock as a big four-digit number. From right to left, the four dials tell you how many ones, tens, hundreds, and thousands are in the number. The correct combination could be any number from 0000 (zero) to 9999 (nine thousand nine hundred and ninety-nine).

That means there are 10,000 (ten thousand) possible combinations — the numbers 1 to 9,999, plus zero! So Steffi's chances of guessing the combination on one try are only one in 10,000! That would be a *lot* harder than guessing what number will come up when you roll a die.

"If you say so," said Kenny. "I'm bad at multiplying."

Suddenly, they heard a *SCREECH*!

A gray cat ran out from between the pillows on the bed.

It raced out the door. And it looked just like the cat in the picture.

"That must be Mittens!" said Steffi. "We just let Emma's cat out!"

Steffi ran after Mittens.

"Steffi, come back!" yelled Kenny.

José started for the door too.

"José, wait!" said Kenny. "Steffi can rescue that cat on her own."

"Forget the cat," said José. "I'm going to look for an old-fashioned ice cream parlor.

"My dad always says ice cream was so much better back in the old days. Now's my chance to see if he is really right!"

Then José was gone, too.

And Kenny was all alone!

Chapter
THREE

Kenny sat on the bed. He wanted to stay close to the time machine, close to his way home. Looking around, he saw a piece of paper on a desk.

It looked like a ticket. *A ticket for what? A movie?*

In large letters across the front of the ticket he read the word *TITANIC*.

Hmm, that seemed strange. The movie *Titanic* was an old one. But not as old as 1912, was it?

Kenny read the small print on the

ticket. Then he noticed the words *White Star Line*.

Kenny felt an icy chill.

The word *Titanic* on the ticket meant the ship, not the movie!

They were on an ocean liner, the famous *Titanic* that hit an iceberg and sank on its very first trip! This trip!

Kenny ran to the curtains. He yanked them open and saw a porthole. And there outside, in the night, Kenny could see the dark, cold ocean. He thought he saw a chunk of ice float by.

Kenny gulped. How long could he survive in *that*?

Chapter FOUR

Steffi followed Mittens up some stairs to a big, fancy room.

She thought she saw something move under a chair. *Mittens?* Steffi bent down for a look.

"Hello? My name is Emma," said a voice behind her.

Steffi stood up.

"I…I know," she said.

Emma was the girl in the picture.

"Really? How do you know?" said Emma.

"It's a *long* story," said Steffi, "but I'm

sorry—I let your cat out of your room. I opened your door by mistake."

"Don't worry," said Emma. "Naughty Mittens always runs away. Mittens has given my mother and me nothing but trouble ever since we set sail."

"Set sail?" said Steffi. "We're on a ship?"

"What a silly question," said Emma. "Of course, we're on a ship. We're on the greatest ship in the world! The *Titanic*!"

"The *Titanic*!" Steffi yelled. And then she thought: *a grand ocean liner, 1912.* She should have known!

"You really don't know where you are?" said Emma.

"Now I do," said Steffi. "We are sailing from England to New York City. And soon we will sail past giant icebergs."

Emma laughed. "Are you a fortune-teller?"

"I saw the movie," said Steffi.

"Movie?" asked Emma. "What's a movie?"

"Never mind. You have to find your mother right away. Then get to the lifeboats. There will be plenty of room in the first boats. But…" Steffi felt goosebumps on her arms. "But not in the later boats."

"Stop! You're scaring me," said Emma.

"Emma, listen! This ship is going to sink," said Steffi.

"It can't," said Emma. "People say it's unsinkable."

"Okay, Emma," said Steffi. "But can we please find your mother?"

"Okay," Emma said. "Mom loves strange stories. But first things first. And the first thing I have to do is to find my naughty Mittens."

Chapter FIVE

José ran up two flights of stairs. As he stepped out of the stairway, he saw the A La Carte restaurant. They had to have ice cream!

José walked toward an entrance with a gate. A sign on it read: FIRST CLASS PASSENGERS **ONLY** BEYOND THIS POINT.

Passengers, thought José. *Is this a ship?*

José jumped over the gate and went into the restaurant.

It was the fanciest restaurant José had ever seen! He found a waiter.

"Excuse me, but what kind of ice cream do you have?" José asked.

"Certainly, young sir. Room number, please?" said the waiter.

FIRST CLASS
PASSENGERS
ONLY BEYOND
THIS POINT

"Um, Room 213," José said, giving his school locker number!

"And your name, please?" the waiter asked.

What name should he give? *Smith is probably a good bet. There must be at least one passenger named Smith.*

Counting Smiths

Some things are more likely than others. And some things are less likely. In the summer, rain is more likely than snow. If your family name is not common, then finding someone with that name on the *Titanic* might be a little like seeing snow in the summer. But Smith is a pretty common name. What are the chances there was a Smith on the *Titanic*?

There were about 1,320 passengers on the *Titanic*. Suppose one in every hundred people is named Smith. Then you might expect about 13 Smiths on the *Titanic*, because there are about 13 hundreds in 1,320.

Actually, the *Titanic* passenger list names only six Smiths. If we divide those six Smiths into the 1,320 passengers we get 220. That means there was one Smith for every 220 passengers. That's not as common a name as we thought, but it's still pretty common!

But then José got a better idea. He saw a vase full of flowers on a table nearby. The flowers were asters.

"Aster," he said.

"Astor," the waiter repeated, pronouncing the word a little differently.

"Yes, Astor," José said, going along with it.

The waiter raised his eyebrows. "Astor, hmm? And your first name?"

"José. José Astor. And I'd like some ice cream—cherry vanilla, please."

"Yes… José Astor." The waiter nodded. "I'll be right back," he said.

But when the waiter returned, he didn't bring ice cream. Instead, he brought a big, angry-looking man.

This doesn't look good, thought José.

"Colonel John Jacob Astor, the famous millionaire, did not bring a child with him on the *Titanic*," the waiter said. "In fact, he is on his honeymoon."

"The *Titanic*," José said slowly. "Hold on a second. I'm on the *Titanic*?"

"The next time you stow away, at least learn the name of the ship!" the big man said.

José tried to run, but the man grabbed him and lifted him like a sack of potatoes.

Chapter SIX

Kenny thought, *What's taking Steffi and José so long?! This ship is going to sink!*

He looked at the time machine.

He could go home right now and save himself. But then Steffi and José would have no way to get back. Kenny couldn't leave his friends.

He had to find them—fast!

He ran out of the room and up the stairs.

Then Kenny heard a sound. A *meow*.

He looked down and saw the cat.

"Mittens!" called a voice behind him.

Kenny turned toward the voice and saw Emma. Steffi stood beside her.

"You naughty, naughty kitten!" said Emma. "You had me so worried."

"Steffi, listen!" said Kenny.

"I *know*," said Steffi. "We're on the *Titanic*."

"It's going to sink!" said Kenny.

"Oh, my! Don't tell me he can tell the future, too!" said Emma.

Emma stared at Kenny's clothes. How unusual they were. Now that she thought about it, Steffi's clothes were strange, too.

"We know the ship is going to sink because we are… from the future," Kenny said. "We came here in a time machine.

Emma laughed. "My daddy says time machines are impossible," Emma said. "He said if they *were* possible… then why don't we ever meet people from…"

"From the future?" said Kenny.

Emma shook her head.

"Well, bingo," said Kenny. "Now you have!"

"Emma, listen," said Steffi. "We can't waste time talking about this. We've got to find our friend, José. Then we have to get back to your room, where our time machine is, so we can leave here. And you have to find your mom. This ship is going to sink tonight!"

Emma picked up Mittens.

And now she looked very scared.

"Promise you'll take Mittens and go to your mother. Right now!" said Steffi.

Emma nodded.

Chapter SEVEN

"José said he was going to look for ice cream," Kenny said. "Let's find a place that serves it."

Kenny and Steffi ran to the fancy restaurant.

Steffi saw a waiter. "Excuse me," she said. "We've lost our friend. He was looking for ice cream."

"You must mean young 'Mr. Astor,'" the waiter said, laughing.

"Astor?" Kenny and Steffi said together.

"The young stowaway," the waiter said.

"He's not a stowaway!" said Steffi.

"Anyway, they took him away."

"Where?" asked Steffi.

"Down below—in third class."

"How do we get to third class?" said Steffi.

"You must be stowaways, too," said the waiter. He took a step toward them.

Steffi and Kenny backed up and ran. They kept running until they reached a staircase, and then they ran down the stairs.

Finally, Kenny yelled, "Wait!"

He and Steffi stopped running. Kenny bent over to catch his breath.

When he looked up he saw a sign at the bottom of the stairs that read THIRD CLASS DECK.

Kenny and Steffi walked down to the deck. A gate blocked the way in.

A guard stood at the gate.

"Lost?" the guard said.

Steffi smiled. "Not exactly. Our friend is in there. He got lost! He should be out here!"

"I can let you into third class," said the guard. "But I'll have to see all your tickets before I can let you back out."

The guard stepped aside.

"No problem, sir," Steffi said.

Of course, it will be a problem, she thought. *A big problem!*

But she couldn't stop to worry about that now.

Chapter
EIGHT

José sat at a table next to some men playing cards. One of the men kept his eyes on José—a guard named Jim.

José knew from the *Titanic* movie that there were a lot of "card sharks" on the ship. These card sharks were either very good, or else they cheated. Either way, they won lots of money from other people.

His guard, Jim, was one of the other people.

Jim lost twice as often as he won.

And now Jim was getting angry about it.

"Why don't you quit?" asked José.

"Don't you know about odds?" asked Jim. "They always even out in the long run. And I'm not quitting until I

Flipping Coins

When you flip a coin there are two ways it can land: heads or tails. If you bet on heads the chances of winning are one out of two, or fifty percent. We sometimes call this a 50-50 chance, because when the chances of winning are 50 percent, the chances of losing are also 50 percent!

If you have a 50-50 chance, you will win one half the time — in the long run. But what do we mean, in the long run?

Flip a coin ten times. Will you get 5 heads, and 5 tails? You might be surprised! In ten flips, heads may win by a lot! Or tails. Now imagine doing one hundred flips. Chances are, with more flips, you'll get closer to a 50-50 split than you did to a 5-5 split. And with a thousand flips, you will probably be very, very close to an even split, with 500 heads and 500 tails.

The more flips you do, the closer you can expect the "heads count" to be to 50%! That's what we mean when we say, "in the long run."

win my money back!"

The men were playing a card game called Match Two.

The dealer dealt Jim four cards: two red and two black. They were facedown, so Jim couldn't see them. Jim got to turn over two of the cards.

Jim won a dollar if he turned over two red or two black cards. But he had to pay a dollar if he turned over one red card and one black card.

"José!" José heard Steffi's voice. He turned to see Steffi and Kenny!

Steffi leaned close to José. "Come on," she said quietly. "We have to get out of here—now!"

But Jim heard her.

"Hey! This boy's not going *anywhere*! He stays with me. And when we reach New York, he's going straight to jail."

Jim turned over a red card, then a
black card. Jim lost again. He gave the
dealer another dollar.

"My luck can't stay this bad!" Jim yelled.

The dealer dealt another four cards.

"Don't worry. Your
luck will change,"

Fair Games

In a fair game, all players have an equal chance of winning.

Suppose you and five friends are each given a number between one and six. Then you roll a die. This is a fair game, because the die has an equal chance of landing on any of the numbers one through six.

Now suppose you and *eleven* friends get together. You each get a number between one and twelve. Then you roll two dice. In this game certain numbers are more likely to win. For example, seven is more likely to win than twelve. That's because there are many ways that two dice can make seven:

First die	Second die
1	6
2	5
3	4
4	3
5	2
6	1

But there is only one way the two dice can make twelve:

First die	Second die
6	6

In fact, no matter what you roll with your first die, you still could end up with seven, but you cannot make twelve unless you roll a six with your first die! So this is not a fair game!

the dealer said. "It's a fair game."

Steffi whispered to Kenny. "Wait. I think this game *is* unfair. But I don't know why."

"Don't ask me," said Kenny. "I stink at math."

"No. You stink at arithmetic," said Steffi. "But you are very good at other kinds of math. Card games have to do with probability," said Steffi. "You can figure this out!"

"Well, Ms. Nomer says that a fair game is one in which Jim has a fifty-fifty chance of winning," said Kenny. Ms. Nomer was their teacher.

"It looks fair to me," said José. "He gets two black cards and two red cards. So he has the same chance of picking two cards of the same color as he does of picking one red and one black."

"Of course, it's a fair game," said the dealer quickly.

"You'd better not be cheating!" said
Jim. "Or I'll throw you in jail, too!"

"Wait a second," said Kenny. "Wait—
I did figure it out! And it

isn't a fair game!"

The dealer stood up. He reached to grab Kenny.

"No!" said Jim. "Let the boy talk."

"My teacher, Ms. Nomer, would say that the only way to figure it out is to look at all the things that can happen," said Kenny.

"What does that mean?" said Jim.

"Let's say the first card you turn over is black," said Kenny.

"Why not red?" said Jim.

"Okay, red," said Kenny. "It doesn't matter. What I am about to say works the same whether you turn over black first or red first."

"Okay. So let's say I get four cards, two red and two black," said Jim. "And the first one I turn over is red. That leaves three cards left."

"Right. And then you pick one of those

three to try for a match," said Kenny.

"If the card I pick is the other red one, I win," said Jim. "But if it's black, I lose."

"Yes, but of the three cards left to choose from, two of them are black. Only one is red," said Kenny. "So you have twice the chance of not matching as you do of matching!"

"Hey, you're right!" said Jim. "This isn't fair!"

Jim looked angrily at the dealer.

"Busted!" yelled José.

The dealer reached for the money on the table.

"Leave that there!" Jim yelled.

"It's mine!" the dealer yelled back.

"It wasn't a fair game!" said Jim.

As Jim and the dealer argued, Steffi tugged at José. She rolled her eyes toward the gate—and the exit!

Match Two

Here's how Match Two works: Jim starts with two red cards and two black cards. They are facedown, but we'll draw them face up so we can see what is going on:

red card   red card   black card   black card

Jim picks any card. He turns it over. Suppose it is a red one. Then here is what is left facedown:

red card   black card   black card

Next Jim turns over a second card. If it matches—that means if it is red—then Jim wins. But he already took the first red card, so there is now only one red card left. And two black cards! His chances of winning are only one in three.

If Jim had picked a black card first, then he would have been left with this:

red card   red card   black card

And his chances of winning would still be only one in three! This is not a fair game!

Quietly, the three of them backed away.

They got to the staircase with its gate and its guard.

How were they going to get past him without tickets?

Then—from out of nowhere—a terrible sound filled the room!

The loud noise of grinding and scraping, of metal tearing.

The kids knew what it was.

"We've hit the iceberg!" José yelled.

Kenny looked around. "Soon, everyone will know about it."

"Hey, you kids!" the guard yelled to them. "Hurry on through now. I've got to run and see what happened."

The guard let them through to second class.

"This ship will sink very quickly," said Steffi. "We don't have much time!"

Chapter NINE

The kids raced to Emma's room.
Along the way, they passed many people
saying that the *Titanic* would never sink.
Steffi hoped that Emma had convinced
her mother to get into one of the lifeboats.

But when they got to Emma's room
and Steffi opened the door, she found
herself standing face-to-face with Emma!

"Emma!" said Steffi.

"Mittens got away again!" said Emma.
"I followed her in here, but now I can't
find her!"

"Emma!" came a voice from somewhere outside the room.

"It's my mother," said Emma. "After what you said, she is in a hurry to get on a lifeboat, but I'm not leaving without Mittens!"

"We can help you find her!" said Steffi. Steffi looked under the bed.

"Hurry," said Kenny. He looked in a closet.

"I've already looked everywhere!" said Emma.

"Everywhere?" asked José.

José reached between the pillows, where Mittens had been hiding when they first landed in Emma's room.

"Have you looked here?" José asked.

He pulled out Mittens. Mittens looked scared.

"Mittens!" yelled Emma. She took her cat in her arms. "You have to stay with me!"

Mittens purred.

"Emma," came the voice of Emma's mother again.

"Come on," said Steffi.

"Come on?" asked Emma.

"This time we're staying with you until you are safely in the lifeboat!"

Steffi led the way out.

When they were near the lifeboats, Emma turned to Steffi.

"Now it's time for me to say it," said Emma. "Go now! Before it's too late."

"Good idea," said Kenny.

"But do one thing for me," said Emma. "That jewel box on my dresser. My father made it for me. I don't want it to sink with the ship. I want you to have it."

"Don't worry," said Steffi. "I'll take it."

With that, they all hugged, and Emma and her mom climbed into a lifeboat.

Chapter
TEN

The ship started to tilt.

The time machine slid across the room. They ran over to it.

"Wait!" said Steffi. "The jewel box!"

The ship tilted further. The time machine was now about to tip over.

"Hurry!" said José.

Steffi grabbed the jewel box.

They all ran into the time machine.

José put his hand on the controls. And he quickly threw the switch.

Chapter ELEVEN

That night, Steffi curled up warm in bed and read as she always did. Tonight she was reading about the *Titanic*.

Emma's locked jewel box now rested on Steffi's dresser.

Steffi decided that she would try ten combinations each day until she found the one that opened the box. At that rate, it would be almost three years before she tried all the possible combinations. She hoped that she would get lucky and find the right combination sooner than that.

Emma's box had 10,000 different possible combinations: all the numbers from 0 to 9,999. How long would it take Emma to try all 10,000?

In order to try a combination Emma had to dial all four digits and then tug on the box. This took her about six seconds. Since there are sixty seconds in a minute, she could try ten combinations each minute. So it would take her 1,000 minutes —over 16 hours—to try them all. If her fingers could take it!

Emma decided to try just ten combinations each day. At that rate it would take 1,000 days to try them all! That's two years plus 270 days!

But every fourth year is a leap year—which means it has 366 days instead of 365—one extra day. There is a good chance that Emma's thousand days will include a leap year! If that happens, it will take her two years plus 269 days!

Steffi couldn't forget Emma, her cat, the noises on the ship, the night on the *Titanic*.

As Steffi flipped through her book, she saw some black and white photos of the ship. On another page, she saw color paintings of the iceberg cutting into the hull.

And on the next page, she saw a photograph of a lifeboat. These were the lucky people, the ones who got to a lifeboat in time.

She held the picture close and saw a girl.

Steffi knew that girl's dress. And she knew that girl's face.

It was Emma! Her mom sat beside her. And Emma was holding something wrapped up in a tight bundle on her lap...Mittens, the cat!

They had gotten into a lifeboat and lived!

Emma had to wonder: *Would they have made it if the kids from Einstein Elementary hadn't been there?*

She'd never know.

Steffi shut the book, put out her light, and dreamed about a new adventure.